THANKFUL FOR
BAILEY ANN

by Suzanne Marshall

LiveWellMedia.com

ISBN-13: 978-1517046163
ISBN-10: 1517046165

This book is dedicated to

BAILEY ANN

Games make me smile
and so do you.
I am thankful, Bailey Ann,
so thankful for you!

I am thankful for sweet melodies,
and lively songs and symphonies,
and soothing tunes and harmonies.

I am thankful for fun artistry,
like sculptures and photography,
and pictures I draw happily
of my home and family.

I am thankful for the parks nearby
with jungle gyms to grip and climb,
and whizzing rides down the slides,
and swings that push me toward the sky.

Parks make me smile
and so do you.
I am thankful, Bailey Ann,
so thankful for you!

I am thankful for all that grows,
like trees and bushes, high and low,
and flowers that bloom and tickle my nose.

Nature makes me smile
and so do you.
I am thankful, Bailey Ann,
so thankful for you!

I am thankful for the food I eat,
for crunchy snacks and yummy treats,
like carrots, beans, and broccoli,
and fruit I pick right off the tree.

Treats make me smile
and so do you.
I am thankful, Bailey Ann,
so thankful for you!

I am thankful for the things that go,
like trains that travel to and fro,
carrying people, carrying loads,
taking us where we want to go.

I am thankful for the sunny beach.
In the sand I dig so deep.
In the waves I dip my feet.
In the sun I feel upbeat!

I am thankful for my little bed...
my place of peace, my place of rest.
Here I lay my weary head,
and dream of happy times ahead.

I am thankful for loving care,
like tender arms that hold me near,
and gentle hands that wipe my tears,
and thoughtful words that reach my ear.

I am thankful for the day you were born.
"Hooray!" I shout and jump for joy!
The world is better with you here.
You fill my heart with warmth and cheer.

LiveWellMedia.com

Suzanne Marshall and Abby Underdog

Made in the USA
Las Vegas, NV
07 December 2021